Used-Up Bear

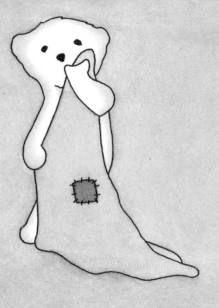

WRITTEN AND ILLUSTRATED BY

Clay Carmichael

Published in the United States by North-South Books Inc., New York.
Published simultaneously in Great Britain, Canada, Australia, and
New Zealand in 1998 by North-South Books, an imprint of
Nord-Süd Verlag AG, Gossau Zürich, Switzerland.
First paperback edition published in 2000 by North-South Books.
Library of Congress Cataloging-in-Publication Data
Carmichael, Clay.
Used-up Bear / written and illustrated by Clay Carmichael.
Summary: Bear worries that Clara will stop loving him because he
is wearing out and getting used up.
[1. Teddy bears—Fiction.] I. Title.
PZ7.C21725Us 1998
[E]—dc21 97-32225
A CIP catalogue record for this book is available from The British Library.
ISBN 1-55858-901-5 (TRADE BINDING)
1 3 5 7 9 TB 10 8 6 4 2
ISBN 1-55858-902-3 (LIBRARY BINDING)
1 3 5 7 9 LB 10 8 6 4 2
ISBN 0-7358-1305-1 (PAPERBACK)
1 3 5 7 9 PB 10 8 6 4 2
For more information about our books, and the authors and artists
who create them, visit our web site: www.northsouth.com
*The art for this book was prepared with
pen-and-ink and watercolor.*
Printed in Belgium

Critical praise for

Used-Up Bear

"A delightful, easy-to-read story about the strong bond that children share with a special stuffed animal or toy. The pen-and-ink illustrations are awash with soft pastels in gentle lavenders and serene blues, adding to the narrative's warmth."

School Library Journal

"Readers will be riveted. . . . Carmichael strikes a chord with children or anyone else who has kept quiet about a source of fear. . . . A joyous ending . . . brings great relief, as well as a message of love and loyalty."

Kirkus Reviews

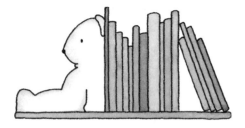

North-South Books

NEW YORK | LONDON

to the little guy in the red suit

One day, after Clara had loved him a long time, Bear looked sadly at himself in the dresser mirror.

His once white fur was as dingy as an old sock. Stuffing showed through the frayed place down the middle of his back. One of his eyes was loose, and his nose sometimes dropped off altogether and skittered under the bed.

"Pretty soon I'll be all used up," he said. "A worn-out, used-up bear."

He had seen what happened to worn-out,
used-up things people didn't want anymore.
They became dust rags.

They were tossed in the cellar where it was dark and spidery.

They were dropped in the thrift box and sold for ten cents.

"Soon Clara won't want me anymore. No one will," Bear said, and wiped a tear from his one good eye.

After that he tried to be very still and quiet so he wouldn't wear out any faster. So when Clara asked him, "Where should we go now and what should we play?" he said, "I think I'll stay inside and rest today."

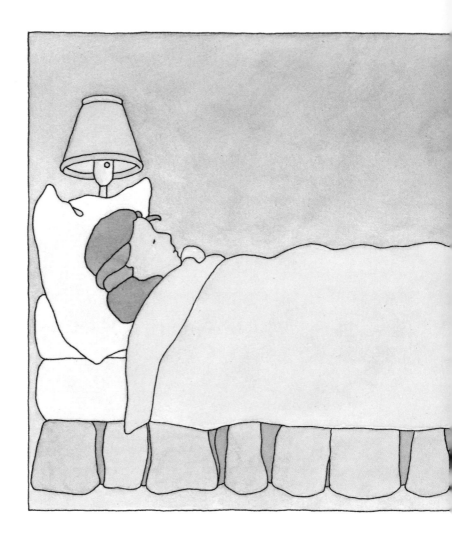

When Clara was asleep, he slipped out
of bed to sleep on the sofa so he wouldn't
use up any sooner.

But he was lonely and cold and the
other animals there made fun of him.

They sang, "Worn-out bear, used-up bear, pretty soon you'll have no hair."

And as they sang they showed off their newness and their fur coats, thick and soft and shining.

They were jealous because Clara loved him best and took him everywhere and hugged only him in the night.

"She'll shut you in the attic," the panda told him, "and the moths will eat you alive."

"She'll take you to the dump," said the monkey, "and the sea gulls will peck out your eyes."

"She'll make one of us her new best friend," said the lion. "Who'd want to be seen with a rag like you?"

And then they all laughed.
Bear crept to the far dark end of the sofa,

afraid every scary thing they had said
would soon be so.

The very next day his worst fears began to come true.

Clara left the house without him.

When she came back, she shut their door and locked it behind her.

When he called to her, she didn't answer him.

He slumped in a little used-up heap in the hallway. "She's made one of the others her new best friend," he said.

He slipped out the back door and waited to be hauled away.

He woke up snug in Clara's bed.

Someone had sponged him clean and white, mended his frayed place, and fastened his eyes and nose on tight.

On the covers was a small package from Clara. The card said:

"For my best friend Bear to wear at night, so I can *always* hug him tight."

Inside was a red flannel bear suit, as soft and warm as fur, with two pockets for his ears, in exactly his size.

He admired himself all morning in
the mirror.

The sofa animals sighed at the sight of him.

"Maybe someday," he told everyone, "you'll be loved enough to have a red suit made for you."

About the Author/Illustrator

CLAY CARMICHAEL grew up in Chapel Hill, North Carolina. She studied at Hampshire College and at The University of North Carolina, where she was awarded highest honors for her poetry.

Her first picture book, *Bear at the Beach*, earned a National Parenting Publications Awards gold medal and was published in Dutch and Japanese.

Used-Up Bear is a true story. When her best friend Bear started to wear thin in his most useful places, she made him a bear suit just like the one in this book.

She lives in Carrboro, North Carolina.

Other North-South Easy-to-Read Books